THE PANGBORN DEFENCE

ALSO BY NORM SIBUM

BANJO   The College of New Caledonia Writing Series, 1972

SMALL COMMERCE   Caitlin Press, 1978

LOYAL AND UNHOLY HOURS   Harbour Publishing, 1980

BEGGARS   Standard Editions, 1981

AMONG OTHER HOWLS IN THE STORM   Pulp Press, 1982

TEN POEMS   William Hoffer, 1985

EIGHT POEMS   William Hoffer/Tanks, 1987

CAFÉ POEMS   Oberon, 1988

NARRATIVES AND CONTINUATIONS   Oberon, 1990

IN LABAN'S FIELD   Carcanet (England), 1993

THE APOSTLE'S SECRETARY   Enitharmon (London), 1993

SEPTIMIUS FELTON   Red Dog Accounts, 1994

CD POETS 2   Bellew Publishing (London), (book with CD) 1995

THE NOVEMBER PROPERTIUS   Carcanet (England), 1998

GIRLS AND HANDSOME DOGS   The Porcupine's Quill, 2002

INTIMATIONS OF A REALM IN JEOPARDY   The Porcupine's
    Quill, 2004

SMOKE AND LILACS   Carcanet (England), 2009

THE PANGBORN DEFENCE

NORM SIBUM

The PANGBORN *Defence*

POEMS

BIBLIOASIS

FIRST EDITION

Library and Archives Canada Cataloguing in Publication

Sibum, Norm, 1947-
    The Pangborn defence : poems / Norm Sibum.

ISBN 13: 978-1-897231-52-4
ISBN 10: 1-897231-52-0

    I. Title.

PS8587.I228P35 2008   C811'.54   C2008-904365-0

Edited by Eric Ormsby
Cover illustration by Mary Harman

 Canada Council   Conseil des Arts
for the Arts   du Canada

 Canadian   Patrimoine
Heritage   canadien

 ONTARIO ARTS COUNCIL
CONSEIL DES ARTS DE L'ONTARIO

We gratefully acknowledge the support of the Canada Council for the Arts,
Canadian Heritage, and the Ontario Arts Council for our publishing program.

PRINTED AND BOUND IN CANADA

for Arcangelo Riffis

CONTENTS

SALVO

Quote me, you hosers, the notion that life
Can't defeat the wise man, the one who's prepared,
And I'll respond in the negative and bring
Chaos theory through your doors.
Disparage fortune as a flaky goddess,
Whim of some poet's capering caprice,
And to the drift that chance tosses at us,
I'll say, 'Patience, you'll get your innings.'
So now rain and thunder. Now the downpour,
And the leaf-heavy branches lift and fall
And hiss, so many sweepings of castanets.
They're beyond philosophy's reach:
The roses blooming against the brick.
But it's as if something in the American mind
Would gut the flowers of their intricate hells
And build camps of detention in the emptiness.

A Suite for the Good Doctor O

Rhymester, bibulous gentleman, son of a Heideggerian,
    You bayou spawn, you've gone and moved to London.
The nearest thing we had to greatness,
    And you went and left us in the lurch.
The Poetry Society in its grotty room
    Drapes a black flag of mourning on its wall.
The closet elegiast weeps through town
    On the teardrops of her melancholy feet.
Incensed panhandlers curse your absence,
    Monarchists now hitting you up for spare change.
But did you go there just to brag
    You've reacquainted yourself with Thomas Jefferson
        and his circle of felicities, his blockheads and scalliwags?
If gruesome farce was what you desired,
    You could've stayed home and switched on the news
And had it direct—the derring-do,
    And tippled yourself into a stupor.

———

Light a fag and pour a drink, you weary feuilletonist.
Wriggle that toe poked through your sock.
You need respite, liberation from a life
    Of meeting all your expenses.
So cast your gaze on a blue sea,
    On an island of hills and olive trees,
On temples and their party-coloured
    Wild-eyed crazies. *Garlanded boats, red-headed girls—*
Was there ever such happiness or did the poets tell tales,
    Felicity the aromas of fish, oleander, the opiate wine,
        harbour festival, in every limb the love-force?
Well, can you say it: e-pi-tha-LA-mi-um, emphasis
    On syllable the fourth? I have one of those items in my mind's

Back pocket, wedding song for the nuptials of fancy and reason,
    For politics all hallelujah and smirk, for the pundits
        of eleventh-hour redemption.
Or, Meredith Owens, you doctor of what I really can't say—
    Did you buy your diploma or did you earn it?—
I'll tell you how a dream from the night before
    Perplexes me, sex with a stranger the storyline.
        —She spoke to me of her troubled career,
            ruined me for satire and verse—
'How was it,' I asked her, 'that the god Zeus,
    Suited up in his swan's outfit, raped Leda, and the egg was made
That housed the sisters Helen and Clytemnestra,
    Pleasure set loose and a lot of hurt?'
'How is it,' she answered, 'that you're clueless,
    Sweet on what I enabled: musty epics?'
Caught out, Meredith, I put it to you,
    You quickdraw, high-end rhymester,
That when I look on the Executive and hear his tales,
    It's purely pain.

——————

Monkey business, Meredith, fraud and parody
    Have hit the jackpot, the hijinks harvest rich.
Shadow-cabinet hums, workers sweeping clear
    The hive of its dead. Brazen birds and jungle cats
        screech and yowl: the audibles of policy.
            Carnivore flowers muster and cross the wide oceans.
And one smells the electoral returns and one blenches,
    Sniffs the whiskeys and the de-lish smoke
Of cigars, takes in and otherwise absorbs
    The rustle of high-echelon nylons and swoons,
        Pentagon, State Department, White House a heady mix.
I beetle along the low road, cheapshot verse my destiny,
    The high broad avenue of poesy all yours.
Yet one of these days, you may hear me step

To a noble subject, atoning for my petty crimes.
You may come across me hard at work,
    Making up for slipshod cadences, lapses of taste.
Hell's bells, I'll donate to every mission house
    Themes I socked away in offshore accounts,
No questions asked. You may hear me saying
    That life's a trip (unless one's becalmed or can't afford
The ticket). True, while some journeys were more epic
    Than departing the Tropicana, gin's cohort,
As I did when teenaged and in search of life,
    To breathe the wholesome stench of freedom, a moral shell,
And got you, Meredith, and Crow and Lunar, for my prize,
    My treks now only take me as far as my books,
The ancients at a loss to tell me why
    Neo-cons still love their infamy.

————

Who needed Charlie Rose, the silk and spice road
    Of talk show circuits? Shifting gears on a hot night,
You'd fly from wine funk to clear-eyed trance
    In a flash, you so much more than your street creds.
But you're now across the ocean, Pimlico man,
    You pimpernel with a yen for *Shane*.
I shamble on as best I can, my six-shooter
    Turning to mush when I most require it.
Do roving ambassadors of American interests
    Have this problem, China rising, the Saudis coy?
Meredith, in lieu of gods, sex, death and taxes,
    In place of how the West was stolen, I'm settling on themes
For which Hobbes would've killed, sons and daughters
    Of liberty mostly s—ts, smug, hoodwinked, ignorant.
I'm stealing thunder from comedy's daredevils
    So as to twit the leadership for the laughs:
'Great country, isn't it, on the rack from sea
    To shining sea?' The hour late, I'm learning new bad habits,

Playing to the crowd though there may come a day
    When the sovereign masses, bored with comic relief,
        might commit a poet to New-Age sacrifice.

———

You've done it, as you threatened you would,
    Traded Fellini for Peckinpah, *La Dolce Vita*
        for *Ride the High Country*, borsalino for sheepskin jacket.
No more salon chit-chat. You're stony-eyed silence now
    Even as, under your breath, you give vent
    To lines of Virgil in Montana-by-the-Thames.
But as for the common man in his Dodge Dakota,
    Delivered from the means of production,
Invited forward, then shoved back
    (Far from the benchmark of the middle class),
It's dog eat dog, tough love for a while
    As when the whores of Athens danced
On the backs of their dead defenders,
    The more manly Spartans breaching the walls.
Yet if a soprano in concert sings 'Un bel di'
    On New Year's Eve, do not think it augurs well
For any new start to come, for a saner Executive,
    For a return to first principles. Do not believe her sexy overbite
    A vestal virgin's, or that, through song, she raises the bar
For values, payback in the eyes of every failed liberal
    And in the leers of every teary-eyed thug.
As she busts through her skin-tight saffron gown,
    Full-blown recitative, churlish and ungenerous
America, at war with itself and everyone else, chills
    Your soul, and you make for the nearest pub.

———

Say that you, for no good reason,
    While swilling your scotch and picking your toes,

You leonine on some item of Chippendale furniture,
  Are reading the works of John Donne.
Turning the page, you find these words:
  'God and man at one in Adam.'
What are you to make of it
  Now that lovers no longer pet at drive-ins,
No longer rub down with olive oil,
  No longer dress their hair with fillets of gold
Or slaughter bulls in love's temples
  Or reach high for Sappho's apples,
    having recourse to 'Boogie Nights'?
What was the poet on about?
Balance? Equipoise? Reformation
  Of a welfare state? Pre-litigious Eden whereby
Adam pronounces the paradisal caveat:
  'There, there, it's all right, and besides,
    this caper will unravel soon enough'?
Inanity is lethal, each day its coup,
  And if to say Helen was just a slut
Heats up the war between the genders,
  What's left of love for lovers is caricature.
Poetry's leeching out of the world:
  Desire, once epiphany, is engineered.
Good doctor, I sorely miss
  The Tropicana times in the lounge of which
A parrot named Mark Antony squawked, sad and wise,
  And the fish in the fish tank wandered stateless
    and the girls wore their hair upswept.

———

In no mood for it, you don't wish to hear
  Of her bad faith, her secret life
In the world's dark places:
  All those vistas of special ops.
Mystery man in your own right,

Bringer of roses to a poet's grave,
Bearer of tears for the lost beauties
    Of obsessive behaviour, you have agendas.
And they're whispered, and it's heartfelt,
    You clandestine in a car park now,
        collar turned up, rhymes for sale.
Otherwise, you're a citizen like any other,
    You singer of threnodies when you shower,
Scrubbing away, smoking your fag,
    Your role minor in some horror kitsch.

————

Meredith, I'm tuning out, poetry my warning hiss
    At countless bad actors, all the world a stage.

————

Wheeler-dealers who have more clout
    Than any Third World potentate
Can't get enough of clout, brass balls percussive.
They who rode the sewage on the rise
    Muscle through the halls of power, mission-heavy,
Each of them a righteous Ahab, so much so
    They paint grim pictures of half the world,
        depicting mullahs and treasonous, liberal hulks.
They produce likenesses and they match,
    In light-repelling mirrors, some hauteur, self-pity, graft.
One knows them from one's high school days
    Living out the pop tune sorrows, sometimes big
On campus, sometimes unfit for football,
    Pimplous, girlless, hosers, hazers, lonely masturbators,
All for Marx or all for Goldwater, politics revenge
    For the iniquities of being teenaged.

————

Serious lyric, life nobly lived? What, Meredith, are you asking,
   I tagging after the golden drinking cups
      of Mark Antony, those that went with him into battle?
      Am I not the son of a lapsed Catholic?
Yes, and those are vultures gathering again
   In the Main Street trees of all the towns,
      gullets long ago cleared of Vietnam.
I put on the comic mask and laugh until,
   My rage grotesque, I reach for the more severe facial
And come up tragically empty, no *deus ex machina* near
   To hand. There's too much scope for fatal missteps,
      populations restive, nature in revolt.

———————

Neither rebel nor late night comic, borrower from and lender to
   Poetry's petty cashbox, it seems I've taken up bingo
And lark with plebs, with fat, old cows who love to laugh
      And show off their skimpy underwear, who smoke and play
         and quote Apollinaire. Do you want some action?
The worst of dreams, it was the best of nightmares
   In which, in the spirit of conciliation, I offered myself
To those cackling darlings. Oh yes, I'll let down my hair,
   But no way, Meredith, will I paint my toes.
I suppose, good doctor, I most resemble
   A mild epicurean of another age, disinclined
      to mix it up with the heavies of a power grab.
They for whom the republic is nothing more
   Than a lemon to squeeze, have been squeezing it
Since their college days, mean enough to ensure
   That rivals got the plums, and then, no doubt,
      such patsies would make a hash of things.
And now that you've clocked your sixty years
   Of stellar service, what's your dreamland melodrama,
You survivor of Jesse James's insurgency, Lend-Lease and
   F. Scott Fitzgerald? Bingo, you say, is not in the cards.

You laugh to keep from crying. Time for those
  Spiritual aims of Ignatius.

———

Mary Harman suspects your placid demeanor,
  Your worldly forbearance, unfailing ease
    with our shortcomings, you fancy-schmancy humanist.
Yes, watch out, she's getting that look. She's trying on for size
  The one that begins to bear arms and march,
    mercy and compassion yesterday's jokes.
Then with winsome voice she speaks
  Of her childhood's christening dress:
    once an heirloom, it's a drifter now.

———

Reasons, good doctor? You look for reasons,
  The grand, sweeping forces that overrun
The little things that go hard on empire
  While half the world starves as we gas our cars?
Vagaries of fortune and character
  Over and against some Master Plan
Unfolding in time and space, determine more than we care
  To admit. You could've been born an idiot.
    America, for now, will stay the course.

———

Ventriloquist's Week on the Letterman Show, and Meredith,
  It inspires me. I'll construct a thing of wood and cloth
And it shall be you. Painted mouth shall emit
  Jokes of an 'Euripides, Eumenides' class of humour.
And you'll sing, you'll croon, you'll recapitulate
  This ancient bittersweetness: *Vaya Con Dios, My Darling.*
Nostalgia, you homesick sod, is what I get

From that Bluebeardish TV host: a potpourri
   of Tropicana girls and idle taxis.
And livried doormen and shade trees and catty slaves
   Running errands. It was forever and a day, that Old Kingdom.
The white-gowned, red-headed, flute-playing queen,
   Pigeons cooing at her sandalled feet, remember her,
Who was more than the sum of Bach and samba,
   The sun beating down on a stretch of sidewalk
      between the Traymore, the granite museum?
And young men like ourselves, had we poems to spare,
   Might have believed immortal her loopy Brandenburgian
Grin. . . . You, Meredith, you interned, too, and signed on
   To life's Grand Projects, such as the Committee to Re-Elect
      some poobah of a silver-haired warhorse.
Even psychotropics, jazz, Poe and Pushkin
   Were no distractions to the enterprise. The smell of hot dogs,
Pretzels and perfume as was half the weight of frail, old women—
   Remember? Surely, you remember, and you must've known,
Feared and trembled with the knowledge,
   If not in your thought then in your left toenail,
That such gentility wouldn't withstand
   The putsch, when it came, against the rot.

Horace wrote that what's local is best,
   But Sallustius suggested that a double date
Between a bankrupt treasury and the super rich
   Invites the worst sort of rule to bring on the worst sort
Of change. We expected Beria. We got liberal-apostate
   Policy nerds. Or just read Tacitus and he'll tell you
That as bad as things get there's always Plan B:
   Evil earned rather than inherited.

Dream girl, incommunicado now,
    And the last I saw, with child, broke it off with me like this:
'No way,' she said, 'will I play mom
    To the arts and reason.' She blamed me for her condition.
It was as if a mere look of mine could've done the trick
    In the way Zeus got spoony-eyed, presto, and
        the next immortal hits the pavement, running.
I suppose I can't blame her, yet I fail to see why
    I should be stuck with the tab for war and rapine
And debasement of mind and the demise
    Of General Motors. What's a poet to do?
You say shove over, make room
    For a humble rhymester, head in the clouds, feet in the tombs
        of the princes of the line.

———

Somewhere, Meredith, and in another time,
    Fingers press upon an oud and pluck
        full-throated bass notes. In the fragrant trees of paradise
Peacocks screech response.
One hears the heat and dust
    And the fountains of the caliphs.
One hears the murmurings of sinuous scholars
    In love with books. Or, take Byzant,
    The place and time of which
Would've suited you well,
    Wine goblet in one hand,
Ascetic pain in the other, Christ's neurotic bridesmaids
    Rustling about in their silks, your pecker weeping.
Such an emperor you would've made,
    Sleepily gouging the eyeballs
        out of conspirators, codifying codicils.
Fatalism, Meredith, overcomes me:
    Blowing snow and Executive Privilege.

In a trance I step to the window, and here's piracy:
Starlings raid sparrows for seed.
'So,' I say, 'this is how nature works.'
(And critics wonder what makes a poet.)
And where do empires get to when they disappear?
If you're wondering, Meredith, how you rate
And what the yardstick *du jour* is, consider this:
If your den isn't stacked floor to ceiling with gaudy trophies,
The shrunken heads of numberless victims,
You haven't been paying attention. Servility's back,
Liberty a double-edged sword.

——————

I tell you, good doctor, she's gone to ground.
I'd grown accustomed to my dream girl,
How she rolled her eyes when I got fancy,
How she wrinkled her nose when I slummed,
Saying, 'If you dumb down to that, you're on your own.'
She's missed, her hair unruly, her heart designed
For the hammerblows which faith invites:
laudo, laudas, laudat—those liars.
The times might be bad, might be excellent,
The price of cigarettes gone through the roof,
jujubes nowhere to be found and she always looked.
To her I'm indebted for these words:
That the best in us no longer answers,
the worst not yet finished if it ever is.

——————

Verses to The Admiral

Jack Flowers, expatriate from Bristol, out you go
   With little mincing steps. But each one of them is game,
You a man of action once, intrepid on sea and land.
A world commended to the deeps, another in the chute,
   You on your frigate saw intensity in the Middle East.
It's the place, '48 the year, to which you always
   Hearken back, you now poking through the snow
With poking stick, darling senior, humoured by
   Waitresses and we colonials.

———

Name your poison. What'll it be? Four Aces Bar? Bavarian deli?
You're overdue at the pizza joint. And Clare the waitress waits
   For you, you the 'old man,' you picking your way along the ice,
A dry tear eliciting memory's depth-charge. 'Oh,' you'll say,
   'I was a sport, bit of a rake, man about town, you know.'
Yes, when you'd kissed, how sly you were, that Kim Novak
   Look-alike in Picadilly, Kennedy and Khruschev squaring off,
How frightened you'd been, the fear on her part
   Giving her pause: spend her last night on earth
     in your bed?

———

You woke to the sight of the snow falling and stood
   Over some porcelain, tinkling, the best part of the morning
Spent like that, the arena of your mind abuzz, alarmed, bemused
   With the nonsequiturs of the President and
   the courthouse gang on the Palatine.
And you imagined you breathed the air that fakers
   In every realm of endeavour suck, priests of the sciences
   clucking tongues, partisans of religion wagging theirs.

One breathes the freedom to betray
   But is one made more honest by it?
Your bad luck it's winter, no terrace available of wine
   And girls, no one with whom to get your bearings,
You on the ice stiff-legged, your whims
   The summer of the dead.

———

Empire or nation-state prone to swagger, what do you care?
Whether free on paper and uncivil and on track
   For its second childhood, it concerns you not,
Your dim old eyes obtuse and wise, perhaps,
   Witness to so many seasons spent
In the hunt for solutions to this and that,
   Plenty of accord, fathomless paranoia.
As when a wave, no longer building, curling over, reaches for
   The next to form, so your life, and you know the essence
For a hoopla of passionate delegates, the monarchy fine,
   The prince a bloody idiot. And now the winter maples
And now the snow licked by the wind, and you know
   Where you are. And the love you knew was less love
Than compromise, the love you caught in your sails
   Something of a legend, the glass you'll soon hoist
      the amen.

———

The thing of it is your ordinariness, Jack, and yet, you've been
   To more places than most men, you Phoenician you of the
      electronics trade, you samurai who fought with cocktails.
Time is not time so much as idea. Here's the idea:
   In another world you're not winded, not winding down,
Skippering a pleasure craft, hair blown about. Even so, you say
   It wasn't much—you'd only been restless, fallen short,

The violin your true ambition, the pursuit of history
    The fallback position. Some day, you'll write that monograph
On Xerxes, he another optimist who blew
    His chances on land and water.

———

Jack, it's your birthday soon, the big 8-oh, and Emily,
    Caustic Latin scholar, intends to fete you,
Yes, with bratwurst, cognac, with words like 'carpe diem'
    And, 'Are you trying to look down my blouse?'
And with any luck she'll smack your cheek,
    And sing for he's a jolly good fellow and such
        as might pass an hour.

———

Your hands folded now in rehearsal, in for a pound and not long
    For this comedy, Jack, you're snoozing in the café.
You're whimpering.
What's that, Jack? What's that you say?
    'Here's to you who said you loved me
    whether or no it was all pro forma.'

———

Whether or not, in the coming months, half the world
    Shall be at war—whether or not in twenty years
America shall join the ranks of theocratic states,
    You, Jack Flowers, with festering sleep presage
Your fabulous ruin. And you drift along as the Nile within
    Carries you, you fanned by ostrich plumes,
        Acting Petty Officer of your raft.

———

Bloom of humble pedigree, your head, Jack Flowers,
   Began to droop. But no, you jerked awake, and the waitress
Need not cuff you about, dispatch expected, signallings by torch,
   Some ghost of some father in a cold mist, injuns out there,
      Terrorists. But why the squirrels or pudgy sparrows?
Why the landlocked capitols, so much history written high
   In mountain passes? Why the Kennedys? Rapacious Normans?
    Why the atomism of Democritus?
Why the Optimates? Or chrysanthemums? Or propagating
   Meteors? Or anything at all? What had been the plan?
    What was yours?

———

The Pangborn Defence

The caucuses, backroom cabals, all those sweetheart deals:
    It's justice less than perfect hammered out. It's a matter
For entrenched cheats. Can politics rehabilitate politics
    In the guise of blondes of liberal causes, of law and order shills?
        We'll never know, and Pangborn, you're no help.
The way you whistle and stamp your feet,
    This café your mission-field, mission hopeless,
It gets you ridicule—it terrifies me your loyal
    Opposition. And what with you at a self-obsessed
Six foot six inches, head a beanbag, heart a pincushion,
    Women wonder what your mom went through, giving you
Birth. You're repressed, so much so that, when you speak
    Spittle flies, your jaws all whiplash action. You're meaner
Than you know. You would've been light of manhood in
    Another life, palace eunuch, you slipperless Cinderella
        disabused of love, religion suspect, literature a sham.
True, you're honest, and honest, oh, you're target-rich,
    Wearing out your welcome among sadists,
        your tears flinty, your ducts sacks of salt.
Give a sign, wild man, when you're feeling
    Wilder, more ornery, in a sacrificial mood,
You sleeping with rocks and beasts and weather
    Of secular provenance. And we'll turn our backs
On what's ascendant, our best thoughts but chimes,
    But coloured bits of glass that rub together.
Deem it progress, how we'll wash our hands
    Of 'getting it done,' how we'll call down a pox
On all the houses and envy no longer
    The bright-eyed and bushy-tailed, the rich and their slaves
All of whom, in the best of worlds, soldier on and avow
    It's better to suffer jackals than dream with fools.

———

Overworlds and underworlds—mutually reinforcing—
    Fall short of systemic collapse for now
If only because the bravado needed
    To stage the apocalypse lacks a tenor
And the pure notes a chump might deliver
    Who'd believed and now stands corrected.
The duelling apostles of conference calls
    Trigger parthenogenesis of the dollar
        while you, without mirth, snicker, wise to the scams.
Oh, women mock you. I'd mock you, too,
    If I could stand your company long enough,
Riverbank, cupped hand, holy water
    Bereft of their recognition scene, you master.
God only knows what stump of a cross
    Still has purchase in the muck of your soul,
You, in any case, too tall for it, you on the rack between
    The god realm and the science realm. Don't you know:
        we've only ourselves to blame for our hegemony?
Go, Pangborn, go, be our saviour in a rough patch,
    Lead us far from a pharoah's pique
To a fantasia of milk and honey so that we might lick
    Honey from the wings of flies.
—Go, Pangborn, my boost these words
    Fatal to gallantry, open to surprise.

———

Lunar Cycle

You latter day Edwardian, you Belle Epoque of ugly times,
    You opera man, you student now of temazepan
And tramadol, you, Lunar, with who knows what
    Curiosities hidden away
In what secret cache, you borderline symbolist all blush
    And palpitation, you complain you're disorientated.
I shouldn't wonder, the pills you eat
    For good sound medical reasons.
Or else it's vertigo, a cyclone
    Of doubt and other debris
Such as spins in your commodious head, such as spins in all our
    Heads, some centrifuge knocked from true,
Or that the poles realign, so much so
    Top is bottom and bottom is top,
        truth, any truth, at premium.
So, yes, what's with you, you on King Street,
    Tall hat making of your presence there
A ghostly ship, you looking spoony-eyed
    At the cheesecake of the Café Maja,
Some vixen of a waitress all in black
    Pretending she's interested while you
        necromance with gilded notebook?
Who knows if I can pin you down
    And locate the cult that lurks in you?
Impossible to stop time and space,
    There's time enough for insults.

———

In this whiplash we call a cosmos, much changes on the fly:
    Love's a fleeting glimpse, oblivion the empiricist.

———

Come late to thoughts of power and what its face is—shadow
    Cabinet—I see you, Lunar, Hammersmith lion
      at the edge of a haunted wood. Literature. *Peekaboo.*
And skewered to your landscape, you swatting at midges
    By the Thames, you endeavour to comport yourself
As a realist over a pint of brew. One's fame? One's fortune?
    One's Plan B? A titter in one's glove.

———

Your turf, Lunar. It was the riverside pub. And the 747s
    Queuing to land. And the scullingboats and the mallards,
And the BBC voices, which all of a sudden, went silent,
    As I, Good Morning, America, went on about America.
The world—how it operates, how it goads
    One into believing one counts as if there were
Only one of one and not one among six billion hosers
    Blushing, simpering, awaiting the fairytale kiss
      of deliverance—evidently, this was old news to them.
How it's a construct in gaudy gift wrapping,
    This world in which we're always deluded: old news.
I said: 'And while we fumble with the ribbons, the apparatus
    Puts on a clinic for a steeplechase—the pursuit of power,
      revenues and, incidentally, bliss.' More old news.
I said: 'It's as when Henry Kissinger, his hackles up,
    His skin as thin as rice paper in media space,
His dander up, for an hour's worth of time obfuscates
    The record, and puppeteers the threads
Of the long view, and still his gorge is rising
    as he complicates his aria of détente.' Very old news.
I said: 'It's as when that grindstone voice of his
    Pummels to paste the finest of powders—the poetic imagination,
Or that to which adheres the froth
    Of a cold pint and a breezy terrace.'
Yes, you said, and you would not have another,
    And the silence around us broke.

———

We'll argue meter, you and I,
    The carrot and stick technique of the rhyming gambit
As opposed to blank verse getting blanker
    In the face of the god's cold eyelid.
But in its collective the visored gaze
    Of imperial poets is as cold.
All those yanks serve a master:
    Justice at the expense of the muse.
Look, he's still with us, the old butcher
    Who prayed with Nixon mired in the polls.
Kissinger was always set too deep
    In the high life of the demimonde
For any worm of a radical goose
    With pick and hammer to pry loose.

———

MK Lunar, farmer's son long since fled this continent,
    Are you so removed? Hookers on speedballs by your house—
So much for that London idyll of yours. Surveillance cameras
    Everywhere—so much for a presumption of innocence.
Even so, the show goes on, and you, Lunar, lunar on,
    Your mug on video tape all tea room and cheesecake,
All thunder over Regent's Park. How it rips across the sky,
    Puts din to a din of ouds and conga drums and clarinets
    and squirrelly, vestal blondes. World music, what else?
And you're there, fan, flirt and agent provocateur
    To such spiritualists soaked to their skins.

———

MK Lunar, bookseller, poet, beleaguered in not one but two
    Beleaguered trades, what offspring of what paternoster
        are you, your father once stashed in Lubjianka Jail?

Will you, with gold-tipped fountain pen, adumbrate
    Your critiques of 'Love for Three Oranges,' of Herzog's
'Fitzcarraldo'? Will you take on Stalin and spin along
    In this spinning world? Too politic to say as much,
Fed in Ottawa the ABCs of a world-class scene,
    You left the cold kavetch of Canada for the maw
        of Hammersmith Station, for aesthetic considerations.

You refugee from Psyche's mode of musing (the self-infatuated
    Did her in), would you lick even now her soft-conched ear,
Your tongue set on edge by Old Pale Fire, you plugged into
    Sibelius, you shielded by a wall of first editions
        against the world beyond your easy chair?
Know, and you must know, how, in America, Venus
    Boosts the leisure-works of the one percenters, the richest hosers
Skimming off the cream, buggering their way from aft to stern
        on yachts of state, dead dictators winking.
Know, and you must know, Psyche bearded,
    That vexed and vengeful Venus retakes
Her mislaid imperium, flashes her shaven crotch and pays
    Fickle alliance with raw gain, gives demagogues grist—imparts
To pastors of mild umbrage the shepherdship of electoral souls,
    Every rootedness a demiurge, each of which shall be uprooted,
My poems more and more peculiar:
    That high romanticism can't be but art
        spurred by the need to improve one's lot.

Weather's strange: April in January. South wind rots the snow,
    Unease the unwanted stray in me, and yet the mind is built
        this way: that it doubts, asserts, and is confused.
I try to focus better, as if straining my eyes or grinding my teeth
    Would explain everything from A to Z, from minotaurs to missile

silos, and what America is to Arabs.
I'm hearing things: *Splish, splash, I was taking a bath*
Long about a Saturday night. Well, Lunar, it's a lyric,
And it hails from back then—in the back-then time
Of teen divinities. Neither Prometheus nor Zeus,
but a rebel without cause
was fit treatment for an unfit age.
So, boy, start sashaying, commence loopdelooping, if you
Remember how, begin hullabalooing, twisting the night away
Across the floor in your polished skull
With some Lana Duluth of padded bra, her hands cold and
Panicked, the American swindle always this:
That the women didn't have hairy lips
And all the world shall dance to America's tunes,
A caricature of God
fattening on its heart.

———

Not fame, not notoriety but fire broached the human limelight,
Brought art, brought cannons and bombs and the means to bring
Tourists to the tombs. Fire cooked fat on the altars of need,
Of our contract with the power, human perfectability now a
bust,
The Lunar payback a Lunar softshoe of mute disgust,
The gods sidelined, those guilty pleasures of poets,
Those impediments who impeded the mind even as they
Were the way out of a blocked exit. Rain now rots the clods
Of snow, and sparrows, en masse, emigrate.
Birds trudge from tree to tree with portmanteaus
And exotic language. And with all the jostlings of a crowd
about to upend a client state, they jostle in a denuded lilac.
So it is in the world at large, liberal Lunar turning up the decibels
Of his Shostakovitch or his Handel, as if to say
Here's the fire, here are the gods and other
Mendicants of the mind.

———

You abstemious when it comes
   To setting the family album to verse,
You riverboat gambler of the personal
   With nothing but ace high to bet, no Lunar poem invokes
The farm, and yet, *padrone* showing off his acres,
     you made a point of pointing out the elm.
A live hand, it rooted things: grass, stone and earth and the pain
   Of your father's wartime ordeal. It was poetry's payback
    to those louts with whom you were schooled.
It stood isolate in its field, a dark cipher in my ravings
   Of kings older than Livy's Numa, kings for a day whose blood,
By way of sacrifice, stained the first Italian temples.
    It stood, a pretty image for your parents who had no money.
It was hostage to disease, burdened by human eyes, so much so,
   How haunted it was, heavy trunk and boughs, leafy mass
Its frailty. But then, Lunar, clever Lunar, now
   That you've gotten me to do your dirty work,
    to paint, *al fresco*, some lost horizon, what next?
I should introduce you to the local tarts
   When the famed Lunar visits again?

———

You hear out a mystic and giggle, slip away, and down the street,
   You apply your teeth to a cheeseburger, at one with the cosmos,
And in this way you recuse yourself. And your stomach
   Churns now, and too close for comfort, some slob hunkers
In next to you, he as fearful as you of the dead spaces
   In the video arcade of his mind. What clarity? All is chaos,
A meal, as horror, gestating panic in your bowels,
   And you move on to the pub, and a young drunk heaves
On the stones outside. And you, sheer lunacy, you now worry
   The rising moon with your eyes, *Che fai tu, luna* and all that,
The poet mind as seamed and padded, as many-celled

As the eye-complex of a bee, pollen gatherer. But were a bee
In violation of its curfew, peripatetic in the lunar light
    Beyond the hive, it just might give the scene a pass and pass on,
The follies of men and the state's criminal acts of no more account
    Than a flower ripe for the sack. Lunar, what transcendence?
Violence. Coarse language. Mature Themes. All is fancy
    And most of that is whim. Oh but then there are history's
Chilling facts, science's homilectic verities, as when
    What goes up must come down, unless some rocket gets loose
And then, another interstellar body begins to own it and draw it
    In. Who knows what distant sun has bid on you
With its solar claws? So that, as you work your way
    Along the river, as the light of the moon brassknuckles
Your bruisable gaze, do you muse? Do you knuckle down
        and retch the barbwire lines of a song?

——————

Your eyes made prominent by those swish bifocals,
    You will have read my new verses by now
Or pretended to, will have sighed and dismissed a crazy man
    With your dismissive frown, your shut-eye as far off as ever,
Four in the morning the hour when reason
    Wants a saloon. It seems you can't buy sleep.
Whereas I, unrefreshed I wake
    From a snooze that stole a march on me,
That stashed me deep in carcerian rock,
    Emotions, thoughts and dreams so many irritants.
Rome fiddles, Babylon burns, and the phoenix nest
        is torched, sweet branches turned noxious.
It's 'the international system.' It's banking
    And other arrangements. And the materialism of pimps
And the delusions of whores touch base,
    cellphones shrieking, with the poor.
By now, you've had enough of me, or that this world
    Spins too fast, words so much slippage of the mind.

Will you only look down your nose at my effort,
　　Saying, 'Sorry, mate, tonight, I'm off to Covent Garden'?
So who's on tap to sing *Carmen,*
　　You skipping out on my muse?

———

You are one who got away (there are others and I salute
　　The pimpernels of poesy, the Houdinis of the book).

———

We're not what we seem, you more up on the trends
　　For all I commit to slang, you coming off, as ever, like a Virgil
On crystal meth. And yet when we at loggerheads,
　　A summit of two on a Rome weekend,
Walked where the parrots flew, the pines charged
　　With a double-task: to dignify old chaos
And new trouble, you were but Silver Age.
　　Just your luck, too, that I, your sidekick,
　　　　was but hell's sounding brass.

———

Rome, and the shelf life for the epiphany was now you see it,
　　Now you don't, the light of day patrolling the grottos,
　　　　collaring the old pigments in our sight and erasing them.
It might've been easier back in Kemptville to tell a tale
　　Of some drugged-up biker's moll, red the colour of her knickers,
As she bent over for something she'd dropped: the mints
　　She filched, the life mislaid. John Keats the poet loved,
Was enamoured of Psyche even as he mused on Rome's
　　Outer skin, Venus the goddess of tired things,
　　　　adoration of Psyche now stale and futile.
Yet, say a thing and you say its negation,
　　Thought the natural habitat of a fool.

You, so you tell me, put on your face, another bad night
 Dreamless and sleepless. Who on King Street will you now
  charm
With your fugitive eyes? Pasty-faced drinkers, dour emigres,
 Addicts too much under the gun for cans of worms
  of a metaphysical bent?
At loose ends, I switched on the TV, and word was conveyed
 Of great new ideas to come, such as will vault us into the future
  on the spin of our progress—
And I suppose, down the road, I'll meet soon enough
 The evils of this moment in their disgrace,
And we shout our huzzahs and baptize an hour
 with briefly honourable perquisites.
Even so, the buzzer rang. I released the door and up the stairs
 Climbed smiling women, one of whom was much too attractive
  for her mission: witness for Jehovah the war god.
Lunar, I figured, all things being equal, nothing changes:
 Nickle-and-diming is the human way, and I waved them off.
Why ply with drinks what would ply me with the end
 Of things? And I went to my cupboard and took stock
Of the whisky and crackers, the oil and vinegar of biblical scenes,
 The sea salt and the sweet amaretto of Fellini's whores,
The pepper, the baking soda, measuring cups, and here were
 My laral entities, my puny religion, if you please—
And somehow I was reassured, which is the point
 Of religion, that one has read the sun and moon rightly
As well as the rising and the setting of the stars
 And know when to sow and when to reap
And yet, who am I kidding? my *Georgics*
 But a TV guide to the day's porn offerings,
And Virgil had been a sentimentalist
 In his epics. It's as when one attempts to imagine
The feathered roofs of Cuzco, the terraced mountainsides,
 The harmless erotic pursuits, and is offsides.

———

Lunar, that you play the guitar upside down
   Is diabolical, if nothing else, nothing sacred, not even
      the heavy breathing of your song breath.
If life's old brevity once took the time
   To chisel epitaphs to transience, now we're rushed,
Tentacles writhing in chillier waters: covert campaigns
      and mission quests, memos for a White House desk.
No ground to stand on, all arguments stacked
   With God or genomes, profit margins, loss columns,
With Miss Manners or Mao, with empire or chaos
   And every station in between, so many enthusiasts of change
Bring on this or that apocalypse-inviting fad,
   House-cleaning turmoil, and it's to be swept away,
And it's a long list of sweepings: patsy congresses,
   Dispiriting suburbs, corporate brands, and we'll start
      one supposes, from scratch again.

———

Impromptu altar to empty air it'll be: I'll heap pebbles
   In my backyard, and listen to the wind swirl around
      the structure, believing nothing, Lunar, open to suggestions.
Oh I believe the old poets, you know, and Masaccio
   And Mary Harman, and she believes
That squirrels are elongated rats
   And you and I . . . well . . .
      best left unsaid.

———

And maybe it's true that time and space
   Have no beginning and have no end,
And maybe the President is a caring president,
   Wise to distrust the mind's products,

His trigger finger connected, though, to the synapses
    Of a mad supporting cast. No holy persuasion anywhere,
No balance in any steely gaze, and I'm here in the winter cold
    Stacking pebbles with my eyes, knowing that the Furies are
        pent up, furious.

————

And maybe it's true that space and time,
    Over time, shall have stretched so thin
That gravity shall cease to cradle
    The yelp of a broken dog,
        the yip of a manic *djinn.*

————

It was, Lunar, weak-minded of me
    To allow the dream its event, worse, to allow you in it.
Look, it was only sleep, sleep the thing
    You overrate. And it was gloom, and the cosmos had
No moral compass, not even shaping gravity,
    And it lacked the spongiform mind of a first enabler.
        Would you, Lunar, care to apply for the position?
For all that, I heard, and it was not your voice,
    Heard the baritone snarl of 'You stink of despair'
And so, was uttered the only A line of a C dream,
    And it was my dream and not yours, you picky, fussy
Editor. 'There's not much more to this existence,' I said,
    'Than the cold calculations of the demented.'
I cited Caligula and his numberless counterparts,
    And I babbled the names of suicided poets.
A dictator's slap-down was in the works,
    So many crimes traceable to his genius, to the Americans, too,
Who oversaw his heavy hand, and will expedite
    The comeuppance.

———

Lunch at Crow's house, and then it was six, six after Lorca's
   A cinq heures, time now that I go in nose-crinkling cold,
The palest rose tinge of a winter sky a scorched blue,
   And I go, regret in me that I had said, 'God is grace'
In Crow's house, Crow, thank goodness,
   Not vindictive.

———

Is it *Che fai tu, luna*, and all that, again,
   And we're never to know the answer?

———

Moon, schmoon, it's Sulla, Lunar,
   Sulla the dictator who's on my mind, he whose name conjures
Bloodbaths, the Roman state, however, righted
   In the prop wash of its civil strife, the spirit of the republic
Stunned, so much so it lasts awhile,
   Is an island of crushed oyster shells
Reflecting the white of the moon and the plangency, perhaps,
   Of a lyre. The man, having absolute power, had it all,
And then threw it over, took to his gardens
   For no other reason but that he was drunk,
Swacked on the moon, in love with moonlight,
   That it bathed him though it couldn't divest
A dictator of legacy. Permit me, Lunar, to put in his stead
   A yankee, a sometime poet, the Pentagon's boss.
No? You can't see the man light on his feet,
   Dancing the beguine with his sequinned muse
      on the crushed oyster shells of undeserved oblivion?
You and I, we're supposed to know
   All about looniness: what's Lear in the king
And king in the Lear, and why men with brains in their skulls

And glitter in their eyes, and a capacity
For a masochistic work ethic, why
  They go and they go and suddenly they're gone,
Failed, outmoded, self-destructed paragons
  Of a republican cast of mind.

––––––––

Lunar, what do I care for your good graces, it being your wife
  I don't wish to offend? Besides, it's on the books:
We live at the mercy of a plea bargain
  Struck at molecular levels. Why then bother
With verses or dreams of childhood or altars of wisdom
  When neither muse nor brat nor deity,
Nor you whom we seek here and seek there,
  Mitigate the malice cerebrums such as nature built
Bring us? Who can say what species of incubus shall be
  The child of the Executive now in place, so many people
So much more intently the thing of which they've been
  The parody? Lunar, I wager you, our fathers dead,
That we'll not ever in five hundred years,
  Get the gist of the century in which they lived.
If a thousand years were ours with which to play,
  We'll never comprehend, you and I, the evils peculiar to us
Such as stem not from memorandums of reason
  But from failures of the same, the mind's darkness
    revelations it would force.

––––––––

And I suppose there shall be a history to it,
  A trail such as pathogens leave in the flesh,
    particles millenia old well-kept in artic ice.
And I suppose there shall be annals in it,
  Ones like Tacitus wrote: December, 2001,
Strange prodigies of nature everywhere,

43

And spooks and neo-cons meet in Rome:
　　phantasms, regime changes. Memos fly.
It's bitter cold here, Lunar, the leafless maples
　　Blonde now in the winter sun. The shadow of chimney smoke
Is evanescent on dull brick. If snow covers the Painted Desert,
　　Mark it down to the wants of a *djinn*
Who wishes all principles of the world
　　　　to stem from him.

————

Long stretches of days so thin of light
　　That the single ping of a piano key
Might shatter the joins of day and night
　　And the tra-la-la to spring—does it, Lunar, ring a bell,
You always saying that there's no cold
　　Like London cold, you morally ascendant
　　　　in this matter?

————

Meredith has been and gone
　　With his seven tongues of palaver.
As he met with me in the café
　　He lit the fuse on a harangue:
　　　　'You call this decor a theme?'
Lunar, the sun shone too brightly,
　　Each table an island, each patron an exile.
Sorry murals on sorry walls would be
　　The glory that was Greece. Worse,
Glittering valentines hung
　　From on high, Meredith recalling
How, despite the hazards, he'd been a ringer
　　In the game of love: my, what a woman,
　　　　the haunches on her. The waitress tittered.
But oh, she can't catch a break. Here's a pest—

The old Brit expatriate at the door.
His cane reconnoitered, its tip saying
   As Baudelaire said, *'Ce monde va finir.'*
But will it, Lunar, will it end
   Not with bangs or whimpers but with cheek?
Where's my service? Where's my beer?
Ah, the Poet's Corner. Should I bow
   Or present my posterior?

———

Lunar, we've long since passed the point
   When body, heart, mind and soul
Had anything like true relations,
Each of those items a revival tent
   in which fake miracles occur.

———

You forever gadding about, now Syria, now Poland or Estonia,
   Kemptville even, I fear your next visit, and yes,
Will we, empty ritual, sit around,
   Nothing left to say, things inside us grabbing our tissues
So as to take us down, so as to rid the avenues of our august
   Preening? Tell me again that no living thing lives and dies
In vain, and I'll turn the argument, so much so
   I'll snap its neck.

———

I hear you, Lunar: I go too hard on this, that and the other
   And lack perspective, have no command of heaven and hell
And the earth riled up. To which I say, 'Right you are,'
   I an easygoing man of the quill who'll always hug
      the coast, deepest fears unremarked.

———

Between error and the illusion that one lives a life
    Of principle, the margin is thin, incalculable. It's to say
There is no margin, the ministry of snow outside my door
    Saying so, and the sparrows hear it, and the squirrels.

———

Come on, Lunar, and we'll do the streets,
    Raucous music in our ears. *Ecco, siamo qui,*
        We're there. Well, look at her.
Is she gorgeous or is she gorgeous? Or is her beauty
    Beside the point, long thick tresses loosed down her back,
        she all flab in later years, near grotesque?
In any case, she's a handful now, Marcello in
    Over his head, and there in the fountain, she anoints him
Lieutenant of the revel. But critics, Lunar, hairsplitting fools,
    They only see in this scene moral drift. They don't get it:
How this pair owe nothing to liberal hearts gone weak,
    Owe zilch to the platitudes that burden truth,
Owe even less to the hour's bullies, are pagan and free,
    However briefly. For in another life, Mayakovsky,
The bridal veil removed from his eyes, blows out his brains,
    While Leopardi, all on his own, eats an ice and sees it
        coming. *Care too much and you'll care less.*
In any case, you son of a farmer, my oldest friend,
    Washed up on the shores of King Street, Hammersmith,
Still eating pills for a banged-up spine,
    Sleeping the sleep of the sleepless, for all I know,
Dreaming the bad dreams of a cornered intellect,
    Shut your eyes a while. Though it were begun in haste
        and without a plan, I bring this cycle to an end.

———

Genesis

Jehovah's retainers Abraham and Isaac
   In an early instance of divine bait and switch
Solved a conundrum by way of slapstick
   There on that rock, the riddle's answer in the thicket.
High priest of the zoological of which we're but
   The grist, and top-dog beasts, besides, you, Charlie Potts,
You even now would spoil the fun and not let
   History, art or anything like a creed enjoy
Sole jurisdiction of the scene of the crime
   And the stiffs slated for the morgue.

———

You've been busy, you no slouch,
   Poet, historian, mountain climber, politician.
But realtor? Were you born with the knack?
   Did you have money to burn
      or did you take a course?
And what if the American century
   abides for the next thousand years?

———

Fantasia for Harriet O'Riley

You woke, you say, as a dancer, and went
From your bed to the dresser on your toes, and you wept,
    Coming to the light, falling away from sleep,
        paradise so much darker than what you'd dreamed.
You bit your tongue hard, and you tell me of it
    Here in the café, and your tongue smarts
Like something the devil grew in you
    That inconveniences and embarrasses.
You exiled your husband to a separate room
    Where he can rot in hell for all you care,
He a snorer, a drunk, a bitter gadfly,
    You ever so cheerful in the shadow of God.
You fled the house, you sailing with birds,
    With squirrels and cats, with fences and flowers-to-be,
With trusting dogs—with vines and shrubs and urges,
    And you have an urge, you who resist nothing,
        to speak of garbage trucks and allergies.
Is there hope for you, you spirit-crushed woman,
    All of us meat for the grinder, flu going around,
You handsome enough to still get the eye,
    Well-spoken for this end of town, laughter nervous?
Ingenue who was rooked and gets over it,
    Sailing down the street with all the tribes,
You look for joints to smoke, drinks to extract
    From every Johnny at loose ends.
And you pray for their souls under your breath,
    And from the same place wish them the worst.

———

Answering Crow

It's a good time, Crow, for a poetic bit,
  Eclogue of sad sack blooms in urban idyll,
Dunkin Donut rubes in their fresh air smoking lounge
  A deadender's conclave, dark clouds on the approach,
    you taking up verse again after a long silence.
—Now thunder breaks upon the realm,
        the air poised to turn, leaves hanging limp—
At the forefront of nowhere, Crow,
  Square away your desk, command centre
    for the enterprise of canard and squib.
But do you have words for the choice speech
  Of petty pushers and pettier thieves,
Every other word of theirs an expletive
  Upside the heads of idiots who couldn't
Find their precious arses in a blizzard
  Much less operate motor vehicles?
Or will your thoughts, by way of preference, prefer to favour
  The girls of summer in their frocks
Over zealots and dirty tricks, the arms of government
  Hardly the arms of wanton embrace, selectively
Affectionate? Sausage makers who stuff a carcass
  With the republic's spirit and then fleece
Us all, and then say they're heroes riding
  The winds of war and market, affix them
With a word or two and a shrug
  To the crucifixes of their malfeasance.
Do it, and old Jack Flowers, cute contumely,
  Who haunts cafés like a hanging judge
Might believe there's something, after all,
  To the poetry of the docket. But what's this?
Sunshine now? Ruckus of starling and chatter
  Of sparrow? Well then, Crow, you have been busy,

Been at it, putting allure to the girls of summer
   Who are the memory of a memory that never was,
The storm brief but vicious through which I snoozed,
   The hounds I dreamed, their quarry buckling to its knees.

———

The pale geraniums coy in a breeze,
   The dark green canopies of the maples—
Here's my outdoor theatre, Crow,
   Of campaigning tragedians. But late last evening in the heat,
My neighbour comes down the swirling stairs
   To my loge chair, and she shows me, what,
A bursting peach, and I was slow to register
   The symbolism. Still, she's a stern Amazon, and she's a loon,
Mystic of franchise parking lots
   Who'll speak your name in full, who'll dock you points
      should you badmouth bagpipes and the supernatural.
Meanwhile in the shadows of the leaves,
   In those places that betray the eye
To the old grottos of the mind,
   Fauns, satyrs and assorted spooks, a procession of patriots
Grabbed hold of each other's tails, and yes,
   They weren't ancients deep in their sighs,
Just people we know of ripening mischief, of sex, politics
   And pandering truth, feeling no pain, in agony.

———

Crow, when you contemplate eternal things
   And the balding patch on your noble head
And the destruction of your social class
   And the suicide of language,
Remember that the Optimates of America know
   The mind masters less than it thinks it does,

That the sane love their orderly mentations
    More than they admire untidy justice, the demented owly
        with dementias, and we swear by our grotty certainties.
But to say we're but transience in a comfort zone
    Only dignifies the standards at work in us
        of pathos, of decay and gas, and what's forever and a day
Are those tax cuts for the rich. Intellectual noises,
    Intellectual surrenders—it's what we've been, fallen short
        of every Hall of Fame and hollow yardstick.
And oh, that we're lovers and carnivorous,
    Consumers of cheesy movies and worse—
I suppose that gets us a vote in some circles
    Among people who once thought they cared,
Whose eyes are listless, whose ears are shot,
    And yet they'll tell you poets are heroes
        and they'll hand you a bullet with your name on it.
High noon that looms in the shadows
    For the heart, mind and soul of a nation
Between apostles of power and dying dreams,
We're stuck with it, Crow,
        and it cramps everything.

———

You, Crow, harassed and harried,
    Have put your house up for sale,
Soon to clear the area as if it's possible
    To shed the isms and leave a fray behind.
But do you think that by a ruse as obvious as this
    You'll outfox the hounds you'll never shake
Who write the new texts, who formulate
    The new opprobriums, the new laws
        and design the new penalties for error?

———

Crow, a satyr play—as follows:

That these sparrows, these tiny thugs
 With eyes of paradise shrieking their shrill heads off
Crouch and prepare to depart my porch
 For an outpost maple down the lane. *Fare thee well.*
That a player of the oud, the sky untroubled,
 Strikes a moody note, then strikes a plethora
Of plummy notes, and I hold my breath,
 Calculate, and otherwise, measure, give a thought
To the distance between perdition and bliss
 Which is nil, zip and void. No happy outcome.
And Crow, it means that this scrap of theatre
 Built of birds and leaves and butterflies,
The odd zinnia up against cruel buffoons
 Or every Cyclops drunk on political swill
 is a false bill of goods. No happy outcome.
And a musician's thumb, though it would in frolic
 Climb up and down the unseen, ivory stairs of heaven,
 strikes the melancholy and the warning.

———

The penultimate application of intellect, Crow—
 To deport one's enemies from the realm
And grab their holdings—is a game that has pedigree,
 history a barren island, consolations in scant supply.
Ask Augustus. Ask Lenin. Inquire of a talk-show host.
Or put it to your cat, regal eminence
 Who regards you with bemusement,
This sleek autocrator of your marriage bed,
 Of your livingroom couch, of your backyard—ask him
Why such lack of sympathy for the perils of doubt
 And equivocation, of liberality—and if looks could kill, Crow,
 you'd have your answer, you living on sufferance.

He sleeps his cat sleep. You worry verse.
Some task, to dress failure as success.

———

Hard-eyed sparrows and soft-eyed dogs,
  Zig-zagging insects in the air—here it is, Crow,
The early evening hour, the neighbourhood settling down
  To bloodbaths, the wind in its bower of lilacs,
    barbecues lit, laundry on the lines.
Whisky, Crow, and I'm in the zone, and soon a sky
  Of modest expanse, pinhole stars, et cetera, shall
Appear. The aspirations of a populace—
  That it gets its plate of meat, its grog and prime time
And untroubled sleep—have long since
  Emerged, yes, from the day's evil thrust,
    and life's good and people like it well enough.
Oh, I just sit here, loyal trustee, the nightwatch
  Of a siege, the TV's glimpsed through windows
    so many campfires of a besieging horde.
—Now here's my voluptuous neighbour fit and game,
  About to bicycle her way through the side streets
    and the melodramas in her brain—
So yes, she who smokes in secret
  Marlboros and that other weed,
Who fears and bushwhacks carpenters of foul speech
  With her steely indifference, who goes from child to womanhood
In a Maserati minute and back again,
  Burning up gas like a Concorde,
In some perverse way she saves my honour
  As she gets on her machine and is away.
Here's the deal: I'm not only doomed, I'm beyond the help
  Of any miracle agency, and she's one of them,
So she's let me know, the verses riddling my head
  So many last stands, Thermopylaes, Alamos.

Red-mouthed in the mapled evening
    Lush with leaf and festive shadow,
Tall and prone to nervous giggles,
    What she might've been somehow misplayed,
Powerfully, she makes that bike go, and it cruises
    As if there's more to living, Crow, than we suspect,
        she a golden girl of a land of shining plague.

———

You recommend silence to loose-lipped poets:
    Less is better, and least is best, so much easier
On the ear. Before I zip my mouth in deference,
    Let me say, 'Twits run the city. Frauds rule the arts.
And homicidal zealots no world can afford
    Caress the console to which we're wired.'

———

Her esoteric fires, barroom sulks,
    Her golden future, storybook past,
This pouting present the grin of which
    Only the White House may temper
With random acts of realism—what, Crow, have I missed
    When it comes to a nation's blooming geist?
The politics, the money markets,
    The sports and the celebrities
That words 24/7 analyze and mull,
Explicating what seethes and brews
    And percolates in the collective's brain—
What haven't we heard of scams and
    Entitlement, of mutterings in corridors?
The histories, the fiction works,
    The around the clock seminars
Of all the heroes and all the villains,
    An endless presentation of

Grotesqueries on celluloid—
One might think we had down cold
　　What boots it for us: happiness and deep
　　　pockets, cheap gas, cheaper thrills.
To top it all, Crow, what I write here
　　Is commonplace, as if, from the Book of Revelations
I steal Babylon, then hand the bewildered slut
　　To whimpering, disaffected liberal dogs
　　　exiled in their own festering sores.
　　—I toss them a bone and walk away,
　　　　weary of the lie there's a side to choose—
So yes, it's personal, and clown that I am
　　Who watched an objection to a state's cold crimes
Pig out on the potluck of lifestyle
　　And then betray life to health,
It's as if I'm forever on a pier
　　Hailing my farewells, tossing my wreaths
At a departing ship—the athlete I was, the amateur,
　　Believer and lover and all round stalwart, one of the good
Guys. Beware the suffering, suspect a dawn
　　Of spite and promise, some anthem
Inviting us to kick off our shoes
　　If only by way of ear-splitting guitars,
And now we've reasons to live
　　And now we're members of a tribe.
And when the feedback, Crow, attains
　　A certain richness of decibel:
Full-blown madness and freefall,
　　Righteousness of coast to coast
Self-empowerment, perhaps I'll join you
　　In your hideaway grandeur.

———

Arcady, Crow, was dementia
　　Of a public and private sort,

For the grass, Crow, was not as soft
　　As the wool of the lamb, and the weeds
Could kill you. Legions tramping down the roads
　　　Might expropriate your fifth-rate dirt.
　　　Goat speech was mostly complaint
　　　　and poets hated rival poets.
And if Augustine said the flesh is vile
　　And we heap displeasure on his head
For saying it, Virgil, following Lucretius,
　　　Called out the passions and named them
　　　　furors. It was bad luck, falling in love,
A crying shame to wind up
　　On the wrong side of Caesar.
Yes, and with fifty-one per cent of the vote
　　　Tucked in his mandate, Arcady not to be confused
With Kalamazoo or Schenectady
　　　But with America the beautiful
　　　　from sea to shining sea,
A man who plays at ranching
　　Can rule like a pasha
　　　and govern as a fool.

————

Unnatural history, Crow, as follows:

Should you, Crow, wake in the night
　　With a yen for corn and wild turkey eggs—should you smell
Gunpowder, Crow, bear grease, war paint,
　　A pack of bog-wet hounds of unprincipled mayhem,
Check yourself for feathers: you may've gone against
　　　The rules, arrived at the limits of natural law
　　　　and human reason, and crossed boundaries.
　　　　(Or else it will prove to be the aftershock
　　　　Of the rye and the cider you knocked back
In your revelry, last evening.) In any case, it's the morning after,

And we sit out in your yard and smoke and exchange
Subdued pleasantries, tribal strife everywhere,
    In every construct made of molecules, in every
        blade of grass and worm, our world tenuous.
Would old Audobon speak so cavalierly now
        Of Corvus Americanus, a bird he shot and drew?
I tell you the news, how some renegade,
    Along with his treasure trove of liberal scalps, has just vacated
The inner circles of government, he the dark angel
    Of plenty of shady characters. A beetle, whirring overhead,
Catches your eye, is plump and vigorous and you say
    Here's a bug that pleases you and God:
Were we to lack its good offices, we'd be up
    To our eyes in fecal stuff. No critter covets its diet.
Well, Crow, cunning Lunar would
    Pry loose my grip on your code name.
Relax, you're in good hands, secure on the pages that I write,
    Almost immortal, sort of celebrated, if not quite
What La Fontaine the fabulist, or Hughes the poet
    Had in mind. What's so much more to the point than an alias,
Monicker, epithet, term of endearment, nexus
    For all that's good and brave and true in the face
Of all that's wrong, than our voices pitched low among
    The zinnias and lilies, peonies, marigolds,
Are the shadows now creeping into the realm
    From a place where the sun has no purchase.

———

Cold and heartless things that tumble
    Like so many ingots from their crucibles,
Their heat like the touch of ice on skin,
    Ideas kill us and buy us protection
From prior eurekas: God or No-God, the combustion
    Engine, hedge funds, the Fourth Amendment.
What, am I locked in a fatal embrace

With the observations of my senses
   and the application of my reason?
Crow, it was nightfall, I a dull glow,
   A sack of molecules on the porch,
The clouds tinged with light and rain, a wind in the maples,
   The air seething with the caress of change.
Are you happy now, now that I spout
   The material basis of the universe?
Shall this orthodoxy please you more,
     Some woman lonely in a window, her man
       watching the Cubs play baseball on TV?
       Do I move to the head of your class?
Well, we're smug in a sleek part of our beings
   Where we lord it over the uninitiated
Who've never heard a truth in vain
   That wasn't spun with lies, the smugness of others
An offence to us, we so many overripe flowers
   Fitful in our garden baskets.

———

Hobbyists of the pleasures, part-time ingenues,
   These women on a Sunday, paunchy and pasty,
     go for broke, bedenimed, high-heeled.
Bells are ringing. And eyes devoid of desire and hopeful,
   Mouths enabled, red and hard in the glare
Of the sun—these are properties of both innocence
   And hell. For the loverboys whom they seek
Can hardly be worth the trouble, they who sulk
   That they're deadenders, too stoned and TV'd
     for the rigours of vendetta.
Oh, they go, these women, and they're each bound for
   That death-defying tryst, and some with time to kill
May stop a while at Dunkin Donuts
   To kibbitz and stall, and here's to them.
Like so, Catullus and Propertius saw it unfold

When bored with the wives of VIPs,
And here's Tara, Crystal or Cindy Cupcake
    Churning up the concrete as she slices in half
The distance between herself and a hoser,
    The wind in her sails, and he'll be swilling beer.
I've always said, Crow, reach around for one's bottom
    And one will grab a Roman, whether of the Suburra
        or a pricier district. We're that close.
Closer still the senators and consuls
    Sniffing orifices for the treacheries,
        gleaning intel, leaning into whispers.
You'll say I perhaps exaggerate,
    Over the top with poetic license,
Have viewed too many movies,
    Have read too much Suetonius, his insinuations
        all vaseline and rose petal.
But leaves talk and women fabulate,
    Men losing stature with the auguries.

———

Black maples, cricketings, bats,
    Drifting voices in the streets
Of boys calling at girls and girls calling back—Crow, the twilight
    Deepened, and it seemed spectral as if it would
        advise some guilty party of its crimes.
Night looked for itself and had no use
    For thoughts of mine, and beyond the cities
Out came the predators. And even here,
    Even in this town, and if one was human, one pretended
One ate on a regular basis
    On account of good governance.
But for this we drained the swamps—
    For this, these manly men of Hollywood looks,
These hard-working moms of elected office,
    And they say the agonies we inflict elsewhere

Means less pain for us who bear up under
  What life dispenses, our soil privileged,
    like some favoured place of burial.
Too true, my observation is petty:
  Life does not ask life for permission to live,
And night slipped into night, moonless,
  And pampered cats prowled the weeds.
And the art Mary Harman makes
  Is darker now, she stung by disapproval of the fact,
To which Lunar responds, *pushing back:*
'Go darker still and then the people
Shall mill around your work like cattle
After midnight, trying, at the trough,
    to swallow the stars.'
—Well, Crow, as you can see
  Lunar shines now and then—
And if sometimes life's been good,
  The pleasures at hand and the means to pay for them,
There are times now, especially after sundown, when
  The night, an open tomb, lonely and flesh-eating,
    looks for blowout wakes to crash.

———

I mourn the cat my neighbour upstairs
  Shall put down at season's end, the plump black pasha
    a Schopenhauerian, pillow philosopher.
    I never much liked it. What gives, Crow?
Down the iron stairs my neighbour came
  To me on my porch, cigarette in her hand,
Grief on her cheek, the nihilist of a feline at her feet,
  And he's old and he's peeved.
Twilight was bringing out the pinhole stars
  To the kitchen sounds of the washing up
In all the houses, and she, shy and grim,
  Presenting herself to best advantage, said,

'There's going to be a death in the family.'
    What, I wondered to myself, am I the village elder?
Clearly, the cat knows, has heard the death knell,
    And even as we speak at this morning hour,
He's down in the yard sniffing grass and twig,
    Fence post and pole for the other cats
And other delights, the trail still warm
    That will grow chilly, and now he's frozen,
        looking for a long time into the wind.
Crow, you most domestic of men, your worldliness derived
    From cuisine and Haydn, laugh, if you must, at my tune.
Now and then we need a reason
    To cry over the humdrum, to bury a bird
Or some other pet, some poem, lock of hair in a crypt
    Of the keepsake earth. It's horrible to say and it's good to know
That something other than rape and pillage,
    Torture, greed and imbecilic statecraft
Shall occasion it, and she played it to the hilt,
    My neighbour, this Greta Garbo hooked on pennywhistle
And bagpipe, and the insincerities of men,
    And will she miss her sour-eyed live-in?

———

You ask after Pangborn and I can't tell you much,
    Just that he took his protest to the capital
And felt ridiculous, he with his copy of Tacitus
    That he held up to the world (as if anyone
Would get the hint)—as if, by stamping his feet
    There on hallowed ground, he could generate
    Legions for the defence of the good.

———

Gilded Curls

Deep clouds of bright sheen amass over the town,
  More rain for lush, lawn patches, Anton,
For the yesteryear Volvos, for the dotty women
  Of this café. 'So much gloom,' they say, and then hear back,
'You're so right, my dear,' and off they trudge
  To the washroom. They bear up under the weight of grey
And gilded curls, martyrs to their fingertips, routine to them
  The tapioca or jello or almond-flaked cake, tea, of course,
With lemon slice—and lo, there are still wagons in their eyes
  And dust, still the endless boneyard prairies, the violent black
Skies. Monsieur Clappique, were he among us,
  He'd swirl the whisky in his glass and say,
'Here are the mothers of all the Rimbauds
  Who do it for lucre and mom's applause.'
You, Anton, son of a mother, Winnipegger in Japan,
  Happy there, your better half born near Nagasaki Road
And the day of the bomb (she puts in perspective the aftermath:
  Music but a stick a chimp pokes with), you just might take
Umbrage at these words, you more sensible than I.
  And how goes the piece for cello and flute?

———

Caesars and Presidents for Avrila Lee

—You swore you'd not die in this town,
   You chagrined now, and moribund—
Oh, you got to Rome, and then Venice was
Your Pisgah, and you could end your days there
A smiling savant, setting suns, wake-tossed boats
   in your smug eye, you misbehaving Fifine.
You met someone, and if not love, here was a plan,
A design friendly to desire. But then, *crumbs*, an unforeseen
   objection
Gummed up the works. Yes, you were about to slip your orbit
When something, *tradimento*, took its evening stroll
All along your spine, and now you've been invalided
   these fifteen years. Avrila Lee, all sores and filth,
   you flop on bed and floor at no remove from here.
The thing is, you know, there was no escaping it,
The coup against life even worse than death
As when some rogue Apollo has Daphne's number
And she must resort to theatre for her dignity,
   And run as she's rooted, sighing in the wind.

———

In what hour does hour rhyme with Schopenhauer?
In what heavy metal canzone do your molecules separate?
Whose laughter is that laughter scorched on your lips?
In which bog do the legions get all slaughtered?
Who'll tolerate your mockery and cigarette smoke?
More to the point, who'll bring you soup? Who'll hear you out
   As you compare apples and oranges, Caesars and presidents?
Like so, the mind *in extremis* operates, borrowing from one age
   To abuse another, nothing on TV but zoos, baboons and their
     troubles.

———

Pangborn brings you soup. Pangborn's a tall ship of a man.
  He pitches as he rolls your way, at your service, you his last
Kick at the can. He'll absorb your buffeting. He'll not flinch
  Before your spit and fury, what with Congress flying
In ever diminishing circles, you know, until it disappears
    Up its own arse—what with the triumph of lifestyle over life
    and art, especially now when you have no life or art.
He'll warm you lunch, his hands all thumbs, his eyes
  Consuming your eyes, your sight-organs overwhelming
Your face—and he'll fetch you your Browning opus,
    And he'll answer, no, he never read *Pictor Ignotus*.
Why, should he have? He'll fill you in on wars of choice
  And the demise of bees. Other news? Well, he supposes
They're scumbags to a man, those politicians, and the women are
  Worse, ice-cold, girly-girls all sleight of hand.
Pangborn is, in effect, a one-trick pony, you his
  New World, his charter, you furious because
    who said what and why is not his mandate.
    He'd have you hush, save your breath.
    Game over for patriots.

———

That said, Avrila, how goes the battle?
    Outside, it's pleasant weather, the wind a breeze
Not gale force: one may sit outside in comfort,
    No need to nail everything down on the *terrasse*,
The price of tomatoes rising for Iranians, they the object
    Of gunboat diplomacy. Will bombs come their way?
Pangborn will have propped you up by now,
    The pillows fluffed and arranged just so.
He'll endeavour to impress you, what with
    That sob-line from *Pictor Ignotus*: *At least no merchant traffics
    in my heart*. Brave words. And they don't apply.

And they don't apply, Avrila, for everything's blind,
   Be it passion, be it murderous intent, be it a gene
Doubling itself—be it infirmity or health,
     Fruition, decay, the virtues seeing but virtue
       while vice sees but what vice perceives.
And so it goes, your rage against chance
   Misplaced and futile, the starry path
Between brain and retina rich
   With maelstrom and serenity.

———

You lump of sores swathed in cigarette smoke, shall I pay homage,
   By way of you, to the human spirit? To what end, you and the
      ceaseless
Pain, you and the mind tumbling with metaphysical bouts
   Of ill temper, matter and anti-matter subverting outmoded
      concepts
Such as good and evil? Your cheek on bad nights nuzzles the
      century,
   And though new, it's flamed out already, unlikely then
To reprieve you, you eleventh-hour mess, from the effects
   Of a collapsing star: regimented hayride of lost souls.

———

If, from the womb, pain expunged you, and you lost
   Your squatter's rights, now you would sleep and sleep
Is absent. In the way the body repels what's foreign,
   America that did no wrong and can do nothing right,
Rejected your tissue, Italy no answer, after all,
   Her tacky modernity, her mawkish ruins,
     her heart-stopping beauty so everyday and banal.
It was different enough, however, that *limoncello*
   Quaffed at the seaside was drink, and how well it went down
On its careless turf. Even so, Avrila Lee, I leaning on Pangborn

for news of you, what now? Grilled cheese? Tinned soup?
    The stone pillows of a holding cell?

———

No, you'll want words less harsh—it's only human—words I'll
    aromatize
With lilacs, with homey backyards, the incessant sparrows riding
    point
on slender branches.

———

Too rich for my verse, authentic outcast, loved by no one
    (unless Pangborn counts), you're letting yourself go, politics
The least of your excuses. Even America's wild men decked out
    In stetsons, bandanas and boots, under the lights
There in Austin City—these balladeers who tip
    Their hats at ladies—are puritans deep down, so much so,
Maurice Chevalier's the anti-Christ, thanking heaven
    For little girls. In my eyes are marigolds and lush pansies,
Some white flower I can't name, in my thoughts
    How Lucretius died of Venus in his garden.
Some deep-fluted white bloom, a few plastic sunflowers
    Gone tacky with age. Avrila Lee, you still-breathing sarcophagus
Of over-large eyes, whether poet or nurse, Frenchman or country
    Singer, what manner of male, hair slicked and voice honeyed
    gravel, shall render you your paean?

———

The dream was so terrible it convinced me we met,
    Your eyes enormous, hair wild, your backbone
A broken snake. Even so, we conversed, and your Tacitus
    Was mine, as was Aretino and what the nuns did to him.

It was noted that Schopenhauer, long a patron of the *Englischer Hof,*
    died in bed. 'The sausages,' I said.

The dream was so vivid I could smell your books,
    Almost sublime the woody scent of them,
Spengler slumped against the Balzacs on your floor
        While Leopardi flew around the room
            like a Quasimodo aching for love.

And the dream was so real, so *there* that it burst
    The bounds of reality in me, you coughing as I kissed your hand.
What chivalry was this, you lighting up a fag,
    You horizontal barfly, Jim Beam the only true prince?

—Well, I could take you slagging my poems, but this, this eerie
        silence,
Shimmering vacancy in the air of a hot afternoon,
    Is worse. I hear the doctors will take your foot,
        Pangborn sullen and mute.

———

Postscript

Figures of stone that I imagine,
Gods and goddesses and heroes
And all the kingdom—birds and monkeys and horses,
Elephants and lions and snakes—slip away into a warm twilight
That hangs in the tall and heavy maples of the street.
The air has no breath, fearful, perhaps, of waking
The parade. Like so, we're drawn on, exodus taken
To a strange horizon. Unusual gravity, death redundant
In its grip. Everything's normal though it isn't,
We alert to every commendation as might grace
Our names, indifferent to celebrity, open to mention
As befits those to whom the misunderstanding
Isn't likely to come, our eyes like party balloons,
Like huge teardrops, festivities intense.
Or is it but a strong tremulation
Of the cosmos at large, those waves that reach us,
The shaking out of some bearded star,
Just as the more earthly world undergoes
Its shakedown? I give you, friends, for your prize a whiff
Of stone and mist, the silence of a city agog, terrors
Real and imagined. I give you sweetly smiling jaguars
And horned cows, the bird-headed staff of judgment
At every corner.

———

ABOUT THE AUTHOR

PHOTO: MARY HARMAN

Born in Oberammergau in 1947, **Norm Sibum** grew up in Germany, Alaska, Utah, and Washington. He founded the *Vancouver Review* in 1989 and published several collections of poetry in Canada and in England with Carcanet Press. A third collection with Carcanet— *Smoke and Lilacs*— is slated for 2009. His *Girls and Handsome Dogs* (Porcupine's Quill, 2002) won the Quebec Writer's Federation A.M. Klein Award for Poetry. He lives in Montreal.